THIS BOOK BELONGS TO:

_____

Jonathan Swift

was born in Dublin, Ireland, in 1667. He served as
secretary to the author and diplomat, Sir William
Temple, then became an Anglican priest, and finally,
was named Dean of St. Patrick's Cathedral in Dublin.
Swift was also very active in politics, though he is best
known for *Gulliver's Travels*. He died in 1745 at the age
of seventy-seven.

Retold by Leslie Kimmelman
Illustrated by Nick Harris
Line illustrations by John Lawrence

Cover illustration by Mike Jaroszko

Copyright © Ladybird Books USA 1996

Originally published in the United Kingdom by
Ladybird Books Ltd © 1994

First American edition by Ladybird Books USA
An Imprint of Penguin USA Inc.
375 Hudson Street, New York, New York 10014

Printed in Great Britain
10 9 8 7 6 5 4 3 2 1

ISBN 0-7214-5614-6

PICTURE CLASSICS

GULLIVER'S TRAVELS

by Jonathan Swift

I set sail for the South Seas

A STRANGE LAND

For some years I had been a doctor in the town of London. Recently, however, business had not been good. So when the captain of the *Antelope* offered me a job as his ship's doctor, I decided to go to sea. I said goodbye to my family and, on May 14, 1699, set sail for the South Seas.

All went well for the first few weeks. Then there was a terrible storm. The ship was wrecked. Six of the crew, myself included, got into a lifeboat and began rowing. Suddenly a huge wave turned the boat over, and all the other men were lost. Only I, Lemuel Gulliver, was left.

I swam as long as I could, letting the tide and wind push me. Finally, just when I couldn't swim another inch, my feet touched bottom. I stumbled up onto the shore of a little island. It was already dark, and I felt weak and tired, so I lay down on the soft grass and fell into a deep sleep.

When I woke up, it was morning. I lay still for a moment, wondering where I was, then tried to get up. I could not move! I was tied tightly to the ground. I heard a strange buzzing noise nearby and felt something alive on my left leg. The creature moved up my chest, and when it stopped close to my chin, I could see it was a tiny man! He was less than six inches tall and was carrying a bow and arrow. Then I felt about forty more of these little men running over my body. I was so surprised that I gave a loud roar. The men scrambled away in terror, some of them hurting themselves in their tumbles from my chest.

I managed to break the strings that tied my left arm to the ground, and pulled some of my hair loose so I could move my head. This scared them even more, and they shot dozens of arrows at me.

Some landed on my hands and body and some on my face, pricking me like needles and making me cry out in pain.

I decided I'd better lie still until night, when I could easily overpower them and get away. But when they saw I was quiet, they put their weapons down and cut more of the strings holding me.

I noticed that the creatures had built a little platform next to my head to make it easier for them to talk to me. A well-dressed man climbed up and began speaking, but I couldn't understand a word he said. By this time I was quite hungry. I pointed to my mouth and pretended to chew. He seemed to know what I meant, and ordered men to bring me food and drink immediately.

As ladders were balanced against my body, a hundred tiny men climbed up, bringing me baskets of meat and bread. Each piece of meat was so small that I had to keep asking for more. The loaves were tiny, too. I could eat them three at a time.

They made sure I had enough to fill me

I washed down the food with a barrel of wine, all in one gulp, since their barrel held less than a cupful. My captors looked surprised that I could eat and drink so much at once, but they made sure I had enough to fill me.

I made signals to show them I wouldn't try to escape, and they loosened my strings so I could turn on my side. They also put lotion on my hands and face, taking away the sting of the arrows that they'd shot at me earlier.

Then I fell fast asleep.

THE EMPEROR

I later found out that there had been sleeping powder in the wine. I slept soundly and very long. When I woke up, I was rolling along on a platform with wheels. It had taken five hundred builders to make the vehicle and nine hundred men to lift my sleeping body onto it. I had awakened only because an officer in the Guards had put the sharp end of his spear up my nose, tickling me and making me sneeze. Fifteen hundred horses, each as big as my hand, were now pulling me toward the capital city of what I soon learned was called Lilliput. It was a very odd way to travel.

We marched all the rest of that day and rested at night. They put five hundred guards on each side of me, ready to shoot if I tried to escape.

Finally, we arrived at the capital. One hundred thousand Lilliputians came to watch. We stopped outside a temple that was no longer used. Since it was the largest building in Lilliput, the Emperor had decided that it would be used to house me. The front door was four feet high and two feet wide, just big enough for me to crawl through. Inside there was barely enough room to lie down.

Meanwhile, nearly a hundred tiny chains were padlocked around my left leg. So even when I stood up, I could not move far.

When I had been made "safe," the Emperor came to visit. He was a handsome man, somewhat taller than the other Lilliputians. He wore a gold helmet with a feather on top and carried a sword the size of a large needle, in case he needed to defend himself against me. The ladies and gentlemen of the court who were with him were dressed in gold and silver that glittered in the sun. When the Emperor spoke to me, I tried to answer him in all the languages I

The emperor came to see me

knew, but he did not understand any of them. He finally left to meet with his advisors and decide what to do with me. If I broke loose, thought the Emperor's men, I could be dangerous. And if I stayed a prisoner, my huge appetite might not leave enough food for the rest of the country.

After the Emperor had left, a big crowd gathered around me, curious because of my unusual size. A few of the men even shot arrows at me, one just missing my eye. The guards, who had been ordered to protect me, tied up the men and gave them to me to punish.

I put five of the quaking creatures in my pocket and held the last one in my hand, pretending I was getting ready to eat him. At the last minute I gently untied the terrified man and let him go. I freed the others too, surprising everyone with my kindness. When the Emperor heard what I had done, he decided to spare my life as well. He then ordered three hundred tailors to make new clothes for me.

Six hundred people would live in tents near the temple and take care of my daily needs. I would require six cows and forty sheep delivered from nearby villages each day for my meals, and plenty of wine to drink, but only just enough to keep me from going hungry.

Last of all, the Emperor proclaimed that six of his wisest men would teach me the language of Lilliput.

I AM SEARCHED

Three weeks later I could understand and talk to the little men. I immediately asked the Emperor for my freedom. He told me that I must first agree to be searched by his officers, so he could make sure I carried no dangerous weapons.

Here is a list of everything the two officers found in the pockets of the Great Man-Mountain (which is what they called me):

• A handkerchief, which looked like a rug to them.

• A snuffbox, which they called a chest filled with dust. It made them sneeze.

• A notebook, which was filled with large letters.

• A comb. The men told the Emperor that it looked like the fence around his palace, but that I used it to straighten my hair.

• A knife, a razor, and two small guns. The Emperor's men had never seen any of these before. They could not guess what they were.

• A watch, which they said sounded like a water mill. They thought it must be a god that I worshipped, since I told them I always looked at it before doing anything.

• A purse. They called this a fisherman's net, but they knew I used it as a purse. The size of the gold coins inside surprised them.

When the officers were finished going through my pockets, they looked at my belt. They said the sword hanging there was as long as five men, and the pouch on my belt held black powder in one of its pockets and heavy round balls in the other.

The two men gave their list to the Emperor. He commanded me to take out my sword and put it carefully on the ground. Next he asked me what the guns were for. I told him not to be afraid, then fired one of them into the air.

16

They looked at my belt

Everyone fell down in terror, except the Emperor. Though still standing, he went completely white. I put my guns on the floor and surrendered the gunpowder and bullets, too. I warned that the powder should be kept away from fire, or it could be dangerous.

Everything was put into the Emperor's storeroom. My glasses, however, had been in a hidden pocket. I kept them there, in case I needed them later.

The people of Lilliput soon realized I was no danger to them. From time to time some younger ones would dance on my hand or play hide-and-seek in my hair. Even the horses stopped being afraid and riders would take turns jumping over my hand as it lay on the ground.

FREEDOM

One day some people reported that they'd found a huge, black object on the ground, and they thought it might belong to the Great Man-Mountain. It turned out to be my hat, which I thought had been lost at sea. To bring it to me, they made two holes in the hat's brim, passed rope through the holes, and tied it to the harnesses of five horses. The horses dragged it over the ground for half a mile, which did not leave the hat in very good condition.

Another time the Emperor asked me to stand with my legs apart so his army could parade through them. There were about three thousand foot soldiers and one thousand horsemen, and they marched with drums beating and flags flying.

I stepped over the wall

I asked again to be set free, and at last the Emperor agreed, as long as I would obey his rules. I promised I would, and my chains were taken off.

I had always wanted to see the capital city, and now that I was free, I could. The people were warned to stay in their houses so I would not step on them by accident. So they crowded at their windows to watch as I stepped over the wall into the city where the palace stood.

It was really magnificent, like a big doll's house. I lay down to look inside, and the empress came to the window, smiling, and gave me her hand to kiss.

Soon after I was given my freedom, one of the country's great men came to see me. We had a long talk, during which I learned many things. I'd thought that Lilliput was a happy and peaceful island, but he told me that was not so.

"You may have noticed," he said, "that some of us wear high heels and some wear low heels on our shoes. By royal decree, only people with low heels are allowed to work for the Emperor, and the high heelers don't think that's fair. It leads to many arguments among the Lilliputians."

Then he told me of a much bigger danger threatening his country.

"There is an island nearby, called Blefuscu, and its people are getting ready to attack us."

"Why?" I asked him.

"It all began a long time ago," he replied. "When the Emperor's great grandfather was a little boy, he cut his finger one morning as he removed the top of his egg. Until then everyone had cut the big end off their eggs. After the accident, however, a law was passed ordering everyone to cut the small end off instead. Those who would not obey were forced to leave Lilliput. They went to the island of Blefuscu and called themselves the Big-Endians. Now they are coming to make war on Lilliput, and the Emperor needs your help."

PEACE IS RESTORED

I agreed to help the people of Lilliput in any way I could, for they had been very kind to me.

I knew that the Big-Endians had fifty warships, and I planned to seize them. I attached fifty hooks to fifty lengths of rope, then set off for Blefuscu. As the islands were only about half a mile apart, I could wade through the sea for most of the way.

I was in the enemy's harbor in less than thirty minutes. When they saw me, the Big-Endians were so frightened that they jumped overboard and swam to shore. I then fastened a hook to the front of each ship and tied all the ropes together. While I worked, they shot thousands of tiny arrows at me. I was glad I had kept my glasses. They protected my eyes from the arrows.

23

Finally, I cut the ships from their anchors. Putting the knotted ropes over my shoulder, I set out again for Lilliput, pulling fifty of the enemy's largest ships behind me. At first the Big-Endians were too surprised to speak. Then all at once they began to wail and scream.

The Emperor of Lilliput was so thrilled when I returned that he made me a Nardac, something like a duke in my country, on the spot. Then he asked me to go back for the rest of the enemy's ships. This way, he could be emperor of both islands. The Big-Endians would have to obey his rules, such as cutting off their eggs on the small ends. But I would not agree to his plan. It did not seem right to me. The Emperor was furious.

Three weeks later, some Big-Endians came to Lilliput to make peace. When they saw me again, they asked if I would come to Blefuscu one day soon to visit. I promised I would. That made the Emperor of Lilliput angrier than ever.

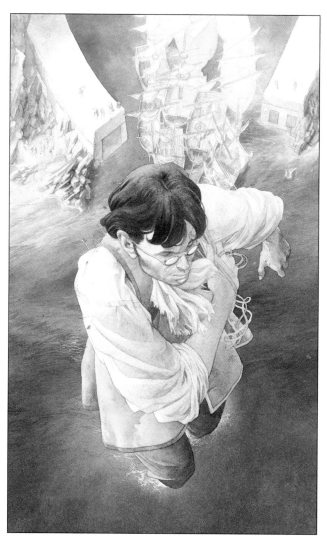

I set out again for Lilliput

I had many enemies at court, such as the Chief Admiral, who was jealous of my victory over the Big-Endian navy. He was also upset that I had been made a Nardac. There were other advisors to the Emperor who thought I was dangerous, or ate too much food, or who simply did not like me. They all asked the Emperor to sentence me to death as a traitor to Lilliput.

The Emperor refused to put me to death because he remembered how helpful I'd been to him. He thought for a long time, then decided that the best way to punish me would be to put out my eyes.

But one of the Emperor's close advisors was my friend. He came in secret to warn me so that I'd have time to save myself. When I'd heard all that he had to say, I thanked him and made my decision. I did not want to be blinded. The time had come to leave Lilliput.

HOME

I went down to the shore and helped myself to one of the Emperor's ships. I stored my clothes inside so they would stay dry, then pulled the ship behind me as I swam across to the island of Blefuscu.

The Emperor of Blefuscu made me welcome there, and his people were kind to me, too. But I knew I did not want to spend the rest of my life in that country. Besides, the Emperor of Lilliput had already sent an urgent message, demanding my return. I did not want to be the cause of another war between the two islands.

One day as I was walking along the seashore, I saw a full-sized boat, floating upside down in the water. I waded out and pulled it to the shore. With the help of two thousand men, we turned it

I stored food and drink on board

right-side up. Then I began to prepare for the long journey back to England.

Thirteen layers of Blefuscudian handkerchiefs were needed to make sails, and five hundred workers sewed them together. Ship carpenters helped me with the oars and masts, and I made cables by twisting together thirty of the thickest and strongest ropes I could get in Blefuscu. On the beach I found a large, heavy stone to use as an anchor.

When everything was ready, I stored food and drink aboard. I also brought half a dozen each of live bulls, cows, and sheep, to show my family. I would have liked to bring along some tiny people, too, but the Emperor absolutely forbade it.

It had taken nearly a month to finish the preparations. When everything was finally ready, I set sail. A few days later I spied a big ship, and its captain took me aboard. He did not believe my story at first, but then I showed him the live cows and sheep I was keeping in my pocket.

When I finally arrived home, my wife and children were delighted to see me after so long and to hear all my adventures. As for the cows and sheep, I let them graze in a park near my house. There they thrived. The cows and bulls had little calves, and the sheep had many baby lambs.

ANOTHER ADVENTURE

I stayed at home for two months. Being a restless man, however, I soon yearned to travel again. On June 20, 1702, I was off once more, this time on a ship called the *Adventure*.

The voyage was pleasant at first. We had a good wind behind us and peaceful seas to sail on. Then a bad storm blew up, and drove us hundreds of miles off course.

We were lost, and running very short of water. So when the ship's lookout sighted land, the captain sent several of us ashore to get water.

When we landed, there was no sign of a river, spring, or people. While the others looked for fresh water near the shore, I walked farther inland. The ground was rocky and dry, so I turned around.

Halfway back I spotted our boat. All the men were already on board, and they were rowing for their lives, heading for the ship. They had left me behind! Then I saw why. A huge manlike creature was chasing them, taking giant steps through the water.

I did not wait to watch what happened. I ran away as fast as I could, up to the top of a big hill. From there I could see the whole countryside. I could not believe my eyes! Blades of grass the size of houses waved in the breeze, and ears of corn as tall as church steeples towered over them.

I walked along what I thought was a main road, but which I found out later was just a small footpath. I came to a set of stairs, leading into a field. Each step was as high as a wall to me, and I could not climb up. As I stood there, wondering what to do next, I saw another enormous man, just like the one who had chased away my friends. I was very frightened, and I ran to hide in the corn.

A huge manlike creature was chasing them

He called out in a voice as loud as thunder, and seven more giants appeared. They carried giant-sized scythes, long and sharp and gleaming. I grew even more frightened. Where could I hide? I ran to and fro, trying to keep out of their way, but they moved very quickly.

At last, just as one was about to squash me with his boot, I yelled "Stop!" as loudly as I could. The man looked down in surprise, then picked me up, holding me tightly in case I tried to bite. I groaned and shook my head from side to side, trying to show him how much he was hurting me. He seemed to understand, and loosened his grip. Then he brought me to his boss to show off what he had found. This was the man I had first seen in the field, a farmer who lived nearby.

The farmer wrapped me in his handkerchief and took me to his house. When his wife saw me, she screamed, just the way my wife does when she sees a mouse. Then the farmer's three children came over to take a look. They were about to have lunch, so they put me on the table where they could see me as they ate. It was like being on the roof of a house. I was terrified of falling off and kept as far from the edge as I could.

The farmer's wife gave me some bread crumbs to eat and cut some meat into tiny pieces. I took a knife and fork from my pocket and started to eat, delighting everyone. Some cider was poured into a cup for me, but I could not finish it, for the cup was the size of a large bucket.

During lunch, the family cat came into the room. She was three times bigger than an ox, and her purring was so loud it hurt my ears. But I knew never to show fear in front of fierce animals, so I pretended to be perfectly fine. And it seemed that the cat was more afraid of me than I of her.

The farmer's baby, however, was much more dangerous. He thought I was a toy and put my head into his mouth. I roared so loudly that the baby

This girl was very good to me

dropped me at once, and I would have been killed if his mother had not caught me in her apron.

After lunch the farmer went back to his fields. His wife put me to bed with a handkerchief, thicker than a ship's sail, as a sheet. The bed was sixty feet wide and twenty feet tall, and it gave me terrible nightmares.

Later, the daughter of the house made a bed for me in the baby's cradle. This girl was very good to me. She was nine years old and small for her age in that country, since she was only forty feet tall! She called me Grildrig, "little man," and taught me to speak their language. I liked her very much and gave her the name Glumdalclitch, which meant "little nurse" in her language.

AMONG THE GIANTS

As soon as the farmer's neighbors heard about me, they came to see for themselves. One of them told the farmer that he should take me to town on market day and make people pay to look at me.

On the next market day the farmer put me in a little box with holes in it so I could breathe, and we set off. Glumdalclitch was angry at her parents for using me to make money. She was worried I might be hurt, squeezed too hard, or dropped, so she came along, too. She put a little quilt in my box to make it more comfortable and to protect me from the enormous bumps of the horse-drawn carriage.

When we arrived in town, the farmer took me to an inn. He placed me on a tabletop and invited people in to see me. I did all the funny tricks I could think of: I stood on my head, I hopped around, and I danced. I picked up a thimble and drank from it, toasting everyone's health.

I was a big success, and the room quickly filled with people wanting to watch. The farmer made a lot of money and decided to travel on to other towns. Over the next few weeks, I was shown in many towns, villages, and private homes all over the country, which I learned was called Brobdingnag. We finally arrived in the capital city, where the royal family lived.

The Queen liked me so much that she bought me from the farmer. I begged her to let Glumdalclitch stay and take care of me, and she and the farmer agreed. Glumdalclitch and I were both thrilled. Actually, the constant performing was starting to make me thin and weak.

The Queen had a little room made for me, with a roof that lifted up and furniture that was just the right size. She had a set of silver cups, saucers, and plates made for me, too. It was like a doll's tea set to her. The room was actually a small box, and it could be attached to one of the giants' belts for carrying.

I ate all my meals at a little table on the Queen's table, just at her left elbow. It was not an arrangement that I liked. Her dinner knife was taller than I was, and it looked very dangerous. And her habit of putting so much food into her mouth at once made me feel sick to my stomach.

Once a week the King would join the Queen and the royal children for a special dinner. He liked to talk about everything that was going on in Brobdingnag and then ask me questions about England, comparing the two countries.

The only member of the court I did not get along with was the Queen's dwarf. He was five times my size, but very short in Brobdingnag. The dwarf was jealous because the Queen paid more attention to me. One day at dinner he suddenly

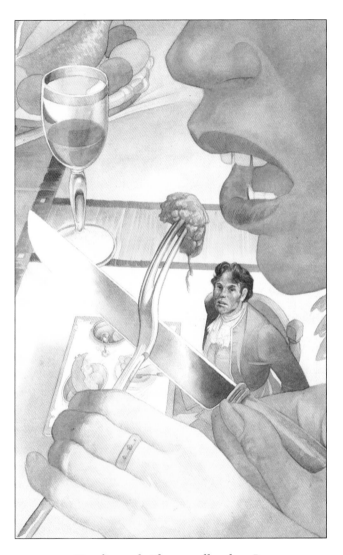

Her dinner knife was taller than I was

picked me up and dropped me into a pitcher of cream. Luckily, I was a good swimmer and stayed afloat until Glumdalclitch fished me out. As punishment, the dwarf was sent away from court.

The Queen ordered a little boat to be made for me, and I often went for a sail in the bathtub. The Queen and her women would use their fans to make a breeze for me. They liked watching me handle the boat, and I enjoyed learning to steer.

Sometimes, however, being tiny in a land of giants was not much fun. One morning as I was eating breakfast, twenty wasps the size of pigeons swarmed in through an open window. As they flew around my head and face, I had to fight them off with my sword.

When the battle was over, I carefully removed the stingers from the dead insects. They were as long and sharp as needles. Later, when I returned to England, I showed them to my astonished countrymen.

Another time, a monkey came to my room and picked me up. He must have taken me for a baby monkey, for he picked me up gently and stroked my face. But suddenly there was a noise at the door, and he leaped through the window and up to the roof, carrying me with him. The servants had to climb ladders to chase away the monkey and bring me to safety. It took me many days to recover from this terrifying adventure.

AN EVENTFUL JOURNEY

One day when the King and I were talking, I offered to teach him how to make gunpowder and cannonballs, so he could win wars. I described how powerful these weapons could be, and the King was absolutely horrified. He told me he'd rather lose half his kingdom than use such weapons, and he made me promise never to talk about them again. If a man could make two ears of corn or two blades of grass grow where only one had grown before, said the King, that would do far more good than winning a war.

Soon after this conversation the King and Queen and their servants set off on a long journey. I went with them in my box. They fixed up a hammock for me so that the bumpy road wouldn't bother me too much. Glumdalclitch came, too, but she caught a cold on the way. When we finally arrived at our first stop, she had to rest in bed for a few days.

I knew we were near the sea, and I longed to see it again. Since Glumdalclitch was in bed, one of the Queen's pages was told to take me to the seashore. Glumdalclitch did not want me to go. She thought it might be dangerous. After a little crying, however, and many warnings to the page to be careful, she finally agreed.

The page carried me to the coast in my little box. I asked to be put down and, laying in my hammock, looked sadly out at the water. I had been in Brobdingnag for over two years now. Would I ever see my home again?

After a little while, the page wandered off to look for some birds' eggs, and I fell asleep.

Suddenly, I awoke with a jolt. I heard a swishing noise and my box seemed to be moving upward very fast. I called out for help, but no one answered.

All at once I was falling

I quickly realized that a big bird had swooped down and picked up my box in his beak. I was flying through the air!

Outside of my box I heard a great deal of loud squawking. It sounded as if several birds were fighting. Then, all at once I was falling. Faster and faster, down, down, down! Finally my box hit the water with an enormous splash!

THE VOYAGE HOME

After I stopped shaking, I looked out the window. I was at sea! I opened the little trap door in the roof of my box to let in some fresh air. Then I called for help, but no one heard me. I was all alone on the water. I missed Glumdalclitch and knew she would miss me. The Queen wouldn't be happy either and would probably send her away from court.

I took out my handkerchief and tied it to my walking stick. Then I stood on a chair and pushed this flag through the trap door, waving it and shouting. Again, no one came.

I sat without hope for a long time. Then, as I stared out the window, I felt a sort of tugging and realized that my house was being pulled along. After a little while the tugging stopped, and there was a noise above my head like the sound of a cable being attached to the top of my box. I felt my box being lifted up into the air. I quickly pushed my flag out the trap door again and called for help.

This time, to my great joy, someone answered in English! He told me that I was safe and that my box was tied to the side of his ship. A hole was cut into my box and a ladder lowered. I climbed up and was pulled onto the deck of an English ship, by English sailors — not giants, not tiny little men, but people the same size as me.

The sailors asked me why I had been shut inside a box. They thought that maybe I had committed some terrible crime and had been set adrift in the sea as punishment. I told them all about the people and country of Brobdingnag, but of course they did not believe me. So I showed them my wasps' stingers, a pair of pants made from the skin of a mouse, and a gold ring from the Queen, so large

I gave the captain a giant's tooth

that I wore it around my neck. As a gift, I gave the captain a giant's tooth, pulled by a Brobdingnagian dentist. It was as big as a wine bottle!

At last the men believed my story. The captain agreed to take me back to England, and the ship headed for home.

Many weeks later, I was back on land. The houses and people looked so small compared to those of Brobdingnag that, for a moment, I thought I must be back in Lilliput again. It sounded to me like everyone was whispering, and I had to learn that I did not need to shout to make myself heard.

My family was very happy to see me, and I was glad to be home. I had had enough adventures — at least for a little while.

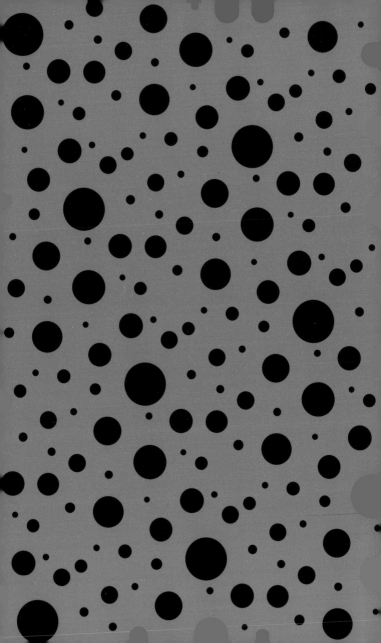